ISBN 1 85854 096 8
Published by Brimax Books Ltd, Newmarket, England 1994.
Printed in Spain.

Tell me a Story

Written by Lucy Kincaid

Illustrated by Gill Guile

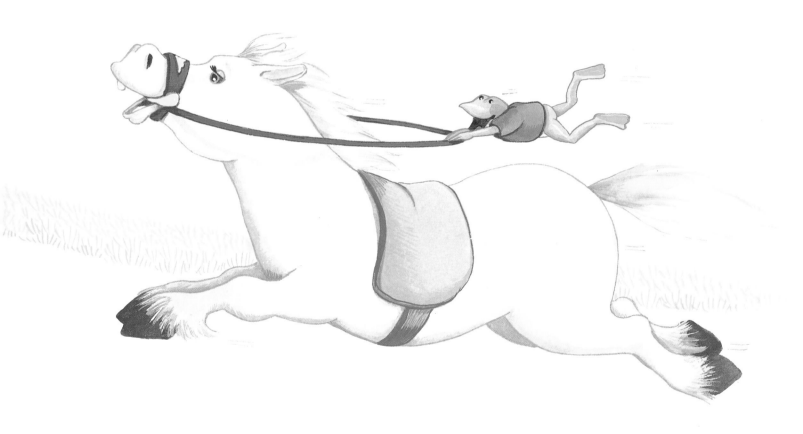

BRIMAX · NEWMARKET · ENGLAND

Contents

Dizzy

It was a warm summer evening and the shadows were growing long. Harriet had been pulling the caravan all day. This seemed to her to be a good place to stop. She looked over her shoulder at Bert.

Bert was looking up at the sky. The sun was already sinking below the tops of the trees. He pulled gently on the reins.

"Whoa!" he called. "Let's stop here for the night."

"And about time, too," grumbled Harriet. She was tired. Her feet ached and she was hungry. It was enough to make anyone grumble.

When Harriet had pulled the caravan onto the grass verge, Bert undid the harness and led her from between the shafts. He pulled her nosebag over her head.

"A horse could starve around here and no one would notice," grumbled Harriet as she buried her nose in the oats.

Bert smiled and said nothing. He was used to her grumbles and mumbles. He knew it was just her way. He knew she would want a drink as soon as her oats were finished. She would grumble about having to wait for that if it wasn't ready.

Bert had filled Harriet's bucket at the last stream they had passed. It was hanging on a hook underneath the caravan. He went round to the back of the caravan to fetch it. As Bert leant forward he heard a strange croaking noise. It was no good asking Harriet if she had heard it too. She made so much noise when she ate her oats she couldn't hear anything, except the sound of her own munching.

The noise seemed to be coming from underneath the caravan. There was nothing on the grass as far as Bert could see.

"There must be something in the bucket," said Bert.

Bert took no chances. Whatever it was in the bucket, it might sting. It might even bite. He cut a stick from the hedge, and keeping it at arm's length, carefully lifted the bucket from its hook and put it on the grass.

Harriet caught a glimpse of what he was doing out of the corner of one eye. She stopped in the middle of a munch and watched. What was Bert doing?

As Bert lifted the bucket from the hook the croak got louder. "Go away . . . croak . . . leave me alone . . . go away . . ." croaked the voice. "Go away . . . croak . . . croak . . ."

Without getting too close, Bert looked down into the bucket. Harriet had forgotten her oats. She was waiting for something to happen. But nothing did.

"Well?" she asked, when she could wait no longer. "Are you going to tell me what it is, or aren't you?"

"It's a frog," said Bert with a smile.

"A frog! In my bucket! What does it think it's doing in there? Tip it out!"

"It's only a small one," said Bert.

"I don't care how big it is!" said Harriet. "Tip it out!" She would have pushed the bucket over herself if Bert hadn't stopped her.

"I probably scooped it up myself, when I filled your bucket at the stream," said Bert.

"You did . . . you did . . ." croaked the little frog.

"Then you should be more careful with what you are doing, that's all I can say," said Harriet. "I don't want a frog in my bucket. You'll have to get rid of it!"

"I'll take it back to the stream," said Bert.

"Oh, please don't do that sir," piped up the little green frog. "I'm tired of living in the stream. I want to travel. I want to see something of the world. Please take me with you. I won't take up any room. You won't know I'm here. All I need is a bucket with some water in it."

Bert liked the look of the little frog. He looked at Harriet to see what she thought. She shook her head.

"Not in my bucket, he isn't," she said.

"We could always buy another bucket," said Bert.

"Oh please do . . . please sir . . . please madam."

A tiny smile curled the corner of Harriet's mouth. She liked being called madam.

"Alright then, but only if he gets his own bucket."

"What about meanwhile?" asked Bert.

"He can stay in mine if he gets out every time I want to drink."

"Oh, I will! I will!" croaked the little frog spinning round like an excited little top. He didn't want to be swallowed by a horse any more than Harriet wanted to swallow a frog.

Harriet looked at him and tutted.

"You'll make yourself dizzy, you silly little creature if you keep doing that."

"But I already am Dizzy," croaked the little frog. "All my friends call me Dizzy. That's my name."

"That doesn't surprise me in the least," said Harriet. "I've always known frogs were ridiculous creatures."

The Bucket

Bert and Harriet set off next morning, as they always did, to travel where the fancy took them. Sometimes it was along lanes, sometimes through woods, sometimes into valleys, sometimes over hills.

But on this particular morning there was a difference. The bucket slung on the hook underneath the caravan had a passenger.

Dizzy was watching the world go by too. Sometimes between the spokes of the turning wheels. Sometimes straight ahead through Harriet's legs. Sometimes back the way they had just come. He liked what he saw.

As the day went by it began to get hot. Very hot. Very hot indeed. Dizzy was glad the bucket was hung in the shade.

Bert took off his jacket and rolled up his sleeves and still he felt hot.

Harriet complained all the time. Bert made her a hat from a piece of paper to keep the sun off her head.

"It doesn't look silly, does it?" she asked.

"Yes," said Dizzy. But Harriet was too hot to care about what he thought. He was only a frog. Every few miles she stopped to take a drink from the bucket.

"I hope you're not going to drink it all," said Dizzy, as he stood waiting to get back into the bucket for the fourth time.

"It's my bucket! It's my water! I shall drink as much of it as I please!" said Harriet, sinking her nose into what was left.

"But I'll shrivel up without water to sit in . . . frogs always do. Frogs need water." Dizzy looked worried.

"The water in my bucket is for drinking. Not for sitting in," said Harriet haughtily. "And don't you forget it!"

"Bbb . . ." began Dizzy.

"Don't 'bbb' me!" snapped Harriet.

Dizzy and Harriet were glaring at one another over the bucket, Dizzy tearfully and Harriet defiantly, when Bert came between them and scooped a cup full of water from it himself.

"Bert!" gasped Harriet, as though she couldn't believe what she was seeing. "That's my water! What are you doing? This is hardly the time to help yourself. There's hardly any left!"

"Which is exactly why I am taking some," said Bert. "Hop in there Dizzy," he said, putting the cup on the grass.

"Hop in! Hop in there!" Harriet looked at Bert as though he had gone mad. "You're giving that frog my water. I don't believe it!"

"I'm sharing it out," said Bert. "Now you can drink the rest whenever it suits you, without leaving Dizzy high and dry."

"In that case," said Harriet, "I'll drink it now." And she did. To the very last drop. That would show them, she thought.

Bert took the cup, with Dizzy sitting inside it, to the front of the caravan and set it down beside the driving seat. There was barely enough water in it to cover Dizzy's shoulders. Whenever he wanted to wet his head he had to curl into a tight little ball before he could get it under the water. But at least it kept him safely damp.

It grew hotter and hotter. Harriet's feet began to drag.

"We'll have to find water soon," said Bert.

"Soon, won't be soon enough, if you don't find it quickly!" said Harriet. "And then I'll be the one who shrivels up and then you'll have to pull the caravan yourself, and how will you like that!"

"Don't be silly!" said Bert. He was thirsty himself.

"What's that frog doing now!" said Harriet suddenly.

Dizzy had his nose in the air, and was sniffing like a pointer dog who has caught a scent.

Bert was as puzzled as Harriet.

"What are you doing?" he asked.

Instead of answering Dizzy said, "Bring the bucket! Follow me! I'll find you some water." As quick as a flash he hopped from the cup to the caravan step, and from the step to the road.

"If you believe that you'll believe anything," sniffed Harriet. "Ridiculous things frogs. They think they know everything."

Bert wasn't listening. He was following Dizzy. It wasn't easy to keep up with him as he leapt over fallen tree trunks and through brambly gaps.

"Wait for me," shouted Bert.

Instead of waiting Dizzy hopped faster and faster. He was certain he could smell water now. Suddenly there it was. A little shallow stream bubbling gently between the trees like a length of silver ribbon. Dizzy dived into the cool, clear water.

When Bert caught up with him he was floating on his back, with a blissful smile on his face. Bert sank to his knees and scooped the water to his mouth.

"What a clever little frog you are," he said, when he had drunk his fill.

They were picking their way through the brambles on the way back to the caravan when suddenly, without any warning at all, Dizzy disappeared through a gap in the brambles.

"Oh dear, what a pity," sighed Bert sadly. He thought that seeing the stream had made Dizzy feel homesick and that Dizzy had decided to go back to his own stream.

But a moment later Bert heard an excited shout.

"Bert come here! Come and see what I have found! Isn't it beautiful?" said Dizzy, almost beside himself with excitement, when Bert, guided by his shouts, found where he was.

"Isn't what beautiful?" asked Bert. He couldn't see anything to get excited about. All he could see was a dented and battered wreck of a bucket.

"But that's it!" said Dizzy. "That's the bucket I want for my home."

"With all those dents? Wouldn't it be better to get a new one?" asked Bert.

"I don't want a new one. Anyone can have a new one. That bucket has character. If I live in that I will have a home of character. Please Bert."

"If it holds water," said Bert. "You shall have it."

Bert carried the bucket back to the stream and

filled it with water. They both looked anxiously for leaks. There were none.

"What have you got there?" said Harriet, eyeing the battered bucket with distaste. "You don't expect me to drink out of that I hope. And where's that frog? Hopped away somewhere I suppose."

"I'm here," said Dizzy, popping up onto the rim of his very own bucket and causing Harriet to jerk her head back in surprise.

"This is my bucket," said Dizzy proudly.

"That's a relief," said Harriet.

"I found it myself," beamed Dizzy.

"In case you've forgotten, you were supposed to be finding water," she said. "But then, I knew you wouldn't."

Bert put Harriet's own bucket, which was brim full with cool water, under her nose.

"What's that then?" he asked.

Without the flicker of an eyelid, or the slightest hesitation, Harriet drank the water to the very last drop.

While Bert went back to the stream to refill her bucket, she looked at Dizzy and his bucket with such a gleam in her eye, Dizzy began to feel nervous, and then she said, "You're not so bad for a frog I suppose, and at least that bucket cannot be mistaken for mine."

Visitors

Harriet had pulled the caravan up onto a windy ridge above a farm. They could see for miles across the fields and over the tops of the woods. Everything seemed very small and far away, and it was so quiet they could hear the chirping of the grass hoppers in the grass.

Harriet was not happy. She didn't like seeing how far she had to go.

The road led on and on, winding and curving, but always keeping to the top of the ridge until it came to a place where it dipped slightly and passed a cave set into the side of the hill. Harriet saw it first, and moaned quietly to herself.

"Please . . . Bert . . . no . . . please . . . no!"

But it was no good, as soon as Bert saw the cave he pulled on the reins. If there was one thing Bert liked more than being on the hills, it was being inside the hills. If there was one thing Harriet liked less than seeing how far she had to go, it was dark places.

"Let's go and explore," said Bert, scooping Dizzy from his bucket.

"Come on, Harriet," said Dizzy.

Harriet looked at him from under her long eyelashes and shook her head. "I'm staying here," she

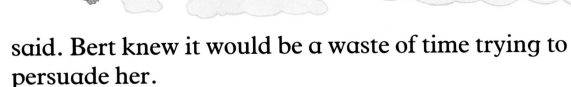

said. Bert knew it would be a waste of time trying to persuade her.

"Don't stray," he said, patting her neck gently. He took the lantern from the caravan and put matches in his pocket.

It was dark in the cave. Dizzy was frightening himself with his own shadow when they heard a loud whinnying.

"That's Harriet," said Bert in alarm. "There must be something wrong." He put down the lantern and hurried outside.

Harriet was staring up at the sky and trembling. Bert looked up at the sky too and saw something which made him tremble.

"It's . . . it's . . . it can't be . . ."

"It is," whispered Harriet. Oh, how she longed to close her eyes and shut out the sight, but her eyes wouldn't close.

"Into the cave . . . quick . . ." said Bert, grabbing hold of the reins and pulling hard. "We must hide!"

The second shock, coming so fast on top of the first, did the trick. Harriet didn't know which she was most afraid of, the thing in the sky, or the dark cave. Her eyes slammed shut.

"What is it?" asked Dizzy, hopping up and down and round at the mouth of the cave.

"Out of the way . . . we're coming in," shouted Bert. It wasn't easy. Harriet didn't help at all with her eyes so tightly closed, but by shouting and pulling, and tugging and hollering, Bert managed to get her and the caravan inside the cave.

"I do wish someone would tell me what is happening," said Dizzy, hopping around wildly as he tried to keep out of the way of wheels and hooves and feet. It seemed whichever way he jumped there was something, or someone, there already.

"Stay there and keep quiet," Bert ordered Harriet. She had no intention of doing anything else. She was already pretending she was asleep and just dreaming.

"What is it?" asked Dizzy again. He guessed it was something important for Bert didn't usually speak so sharply to Harriet.

Bert wiped the perspiration from his brow.

"I'm sorry Dizzy," he said. "But I had to get her inside."

"I can see that," said Dizzy, "But why?"

"I'm not really sure," said Bert, "but I think it's a flying saucer."

"What are we going to do?" Dizzy was frightened.

"Stay hidden and watch," said Bert. "That is all we can do."

"I can hear something," said Dizzy. There was a strange noise like dozens of teacups rattling on a tray. It was Harriet's teeth. Bert pulled her haybag over her head to muffle the sound. They had to be quiet.

There was another noise. A low whining hum that steadily grew louder. A large object like two saucers, one turned upside down on top of the other, skimmed over the grass and landed on the grassy slopes of the hill. A hatchway opened. A figure stepped out, looked around and then beckoned to someone inside.

The air was suddenly filled with screeches and shouts. Bert clapped his hands over his ears. Dizzy took one wild leap into Bert's pocket. Harriet was so startled she forgot to be afraid and opened her eyes until they were as wide as plates.

Hundreds of small figures with green faces and long feet were jumping from the saucer. It was like a volcanic eruption.

"It's an invasion," whispered Bert. "We must do something." But while he was trying to think of what to do, Bert noticed something.

"Are they laying traps?" asked Dizzy, looking out from a hole in Bert's pocket.

"No . . . no . . . they're not . . ." said Bert, his voice beginning to fill with wonder. "It looks just like one of those outings humans have for the young ones. I think it's called a picnic."

"Can't be!" snapped Harriet who had her eyes closed again. "You'll be telling me they're picking daisies next."

"They are!" said Bert.

Harriet's eyes flew open. "Picking daisies . . . picking my daisies! How dare they!" Harriet forgot all about being afraid. She also forgot to whisper.

"Shush," said Bert. But he was too late. There was a warning cry. Everyone ran to the saucer and leapt inside. With a quick whirr and a gentle hum the craft took off and disappeared into the sky.

Harriet shook her head as though she had just woken from a dream. "Come along, " she said. "It's time we moved on." And with no more ado, she pulled the caravan from the cave and plodded off, leaving Bert and Dizzy to run after her.

"Let me tell you about the dream I had this morning," she said, when they caught up with her. And by the time she had finished, Bert and Dizzy began to wonder if they had dreamt the morning's events as well. They often thought about it afterwards and were never really sure.

The Birthday Party

After their adventure in the cave they stopped for the night under a willow tree growing beside a narrow stream. Bert unhitched Harriet and left her to graze.

"Mmm," she mumbled greedily, putting her head down and beginning her supper immediately.

Bert upended Dizzy's bucket over the stream. Dizzy plopped into the water, stretched his legs and swam off downstream.

"See you later," called Bert.

"Gurgle . . . urble . . . gur . . ." called Dizzy from under the water, which Bert supposed meant, yes, he would see him later. Bert had his supper and sat out on the caravan steps. Presently Dizzy came back from his swim and sat beside him.

"Time to light the lantern," said Bert as it began to get dark. But there was no lantern to light. They had left it behind in the cave.

"I put it on the ground when Harriet whinnied," said Bert, "and forgot to pick it up."

"I suppose you're going to say it's my fault," grumbled Harriet. She had eaten her supper too quickly and had indigestion.

"Don't be silly," said Bert sharply. "It's no one's fault. It just happened."

"I suppose I'll have to stand in the dark," she mumbled. She always did stand in the dark. She liked standing in the dark. She only wanted the lantern lit because she knew it wasn't there.

"Do stop grumbling," said Bert. He shouldn't have said it, for with a toss of her mane, Harriet stalked away and stood by herself on the far side of the willow tree.

Bert and Dizzy sat together on the caravan steps watching the moon rise in the night sky. Presently there was a quiet whinny from Harriet. Bert went to check that she was alright.

"There's something moving about down there," she said. "What is it?"

Bert didn't know. There was a ripple on the surface of the water, but he could see nothing else.

"I knew we shouldn't have lost that lantern," mumbled Harriet to herself. "How can I see what's there if we have no lantern?" She moved away from the stream and stood beside the caravan. She had no intention of letting any creepy crawly thing creep up behind her and take her by surprise.

"What's the matter with Harriet?" asked Dizzy.

"She thought she saw something. She's jumpy tonight."

"So would you be if you had no lantern," sniffed Harriet choosing to forget that if she had no lantern then neither did they.

Bert's eyes were getting used to the darkness. He thought he saw something moving across the grass.

"Is there something there?" he asked Dizzy.

"Of course there's something there," said Harriet "Haven't I just told you so."

"Oh, do be quiet," grumbled Dizzy. He wanted to watch the shadows.

Suddenly he began to bounce up and down with excitement.

"It's frogs . . . frogs . . . lots of frogs . . ." he shouted. "Hundreds and hundreds of frogs . . . it's frogs."

"Well they're your relations, go and see what they want," snapped Harriet.

"Alright I will," retorted Dizzy and with one bound he was gone. Suddenly a babble of croaks broke the still night air.

Harriet forgot she was sulking. "Bert . . . save him . . . save Dizzy," she cried, shutting her eyes tight at the same time so that she couldn't see if anything awful happened.

43

"I don't want saving," yelled Dizzy.

Presently Dizzy came bounding back, grinning all over his little green face. "It's a celebration," he sang out happily. "Grandpa Bullfrog is a hundred bullfrog years old today. Everyone has come to wish him a happy birthday and to dance at his party."

"Frogs dance! With those legs!" scoffed Harriet.

"This is their meeting place," explained Dizzy.

"In that case we had better move on and let them have their party," said Bert. "We mustn't spoil their fun."

"But we won't," said Dizzy. "We've been invited to join in the dancing."

"How can I join in?" laughed Bert. "They are all a hundred times smaller than me. I'd be sure to tread on at least one of them."

"That's alright," said Dizzy. "You and Harriet can watch instead."

"What makes you think I want to watch a lot of frogs dancing," said Harriet. But it wasn't long before her foot was tapping.

The frogs danced and they croaked. They ran races, and danced again. They hopped races and they jumped races and danced and croaked all over again. Grandpa Bullfrog jumped and danced and croaked as merrily as everyone else. It was his birthday after all.

It was such a good party that Harriet forgot her indigestion and her sulks. To her ears the croaking of the frogs was very untuneful, but it made her want to sing. To the frogs ears her singing was the most extraordinary noise they had ever heard, but no one seemed to mind. Everyone was too happy.

At half past two in the morning the frogs began their trek home. Some of them had several miles to travel and they had to get home before it was light.

"That's the best birthday party I've ever been to," sighed Dizzy. "And to think, if we had had the lantern it would never have happened."

"Why not?" asked Harriet.

"Because if the lantern had been lit, the party would have been held elsewhere. Frogs aren't silly you know, to them lights at night can spell danger."

Harriet smiled serenely. "If it hadn't been for me, Bert wouldn't have left the lantern behind. If it hadn't been for me the lantern would have been lit, and the frogs would have gone away. If it hadn't been for me there would have been no party."

"How does she think of these things?" asked Dizzy.

Bert laughed. "Because she's Harriet," he said. "We'll go back and fetch the lantern tomorrow. Now let's all get some sleep before the sun comes up and the birds start singing."

New Shoes for Harriet

Harriet was lame.

"Perhaps her shoes are hurting her," said Dizzy. Dizzy thought he had made a joke so was very surprised to hear Bert say, "Is he right Harriet? Are your shoes hurting you?"

"They are pinching," said Harriet sadly.

"She doesn't really wear shoes, does she?" asked Dizzy. Bert showed him the metal shoes nailed to Harriet's hooves.

Dizzy was amazed. "I didn't know that!" he said.

"Well you know now!" snapped Harriet.

"We'll have to get her some new ones," said Bert.

"And not before time," grumbled Harriet. "Does no one ever think of all the walking I have to do?"

There was a field close by. Bert led Harriet into it and unhitched the caravan.

"Are you ready?" he asked Dizzy.

"Ready? What for?" asked Dizzy.

"We must take Harriet to the blacksmith," said Bert.

"But why? Can't you buy her some new shoes and bring them back here?" Dizzy didn't understand any of this.

"No," laughed Bert. "They have to be specially fitted."

Bert sat Dizzy on his shoulder and they set off. It seemed very odd walking along the country lanes with Harriet hobbling along beside them and with the caravan left behind in a field. Dizzy kept looking back to make sure they really had left it behind. He missed it's rumbling wheels.

Harriet missed it too. "Hurry up," she said. "The quicker this is done the better."

They found a blacksmith in the very first village they came to. Harriet stayed quite calm as the blacksmith hammered the new shoes into place, after all she was used to it. But Dizzy wasn't. He winced each time the hammer struck a nail.

"Poor old Harriet," he kept saying, over and over again. "Poor old Harriet."

"I'm not poor or old," she tutted grandly. "I'll ask you to mind your manners."

They began the long walk back to the caravan. Now it was Bert's turn to have aching feet. His turn to limp.

"Get onto my back Bert," said Harriet. Now that her feet felt better her temper had improved. "You can ride home."

Bert pulled himself up onto her back. Dizzy nearly swooned with excitement at being so high in the air.

Harriet set off at a brisk trot. Clippity clop, clippity clop, clippity clop.

"Isn't it exciting!" called Dizzy, bouncing up with every clip and down with every clop.

After a while Bert whispered quietly to Dizzy. "I'm sure we should have reached the caravan by now. We must have taken a wrong turning somewhere."

"We can't have," said Dizzy. "Harriet has such a good sense of direction."

"It isn't always reliable," muttered Bert. "Not when she gets excited and look how excited she is now." Harriet was holding her head high and her ears were twitching. Dizzy suddenly noticed just how fast she was moving.

"What are we going to do?" he asked.

"Stop her and think," said Bert. "Whoa there!" he called, pulling hard on her mane.

"Yes . . ." she said sweetly, turning her head to look at him, her eyes sparkling with excitement. "What do you want?"

Bert tried to put it carefully. He didn't want to hurt her feelings. "ER . . . er . . ." he said. "I . . . I . . ."

53

"We're lost," said Dizzy bluntly.

"Lost?" Harriet looked at Dizzy and giggled. "Don't be silly. How can we be lost. We're travellers."

"Travellers without a caravan!" retorted Dizzy. "We've lost the caravan."

Harriet looked at Bert to see how serious he was being. Perhaps they were playing a joke on her.

"Well," said Bert, "either the caravan's lost, or we are."

They wandered up lanes, and took short cuts across fields. They crossed two streams. And still they found no caravan. Then to make matters worse, far worse, it began to get dark.

"I want my bucket!" wailed Dizzy. "Where's my bucket?"

"Oh, stop it, you silly little frog," grumbled Harriet. "I want my caravan, but I'm not making a fuss about it."

Bert said nothing at all. He thought it wiser not to.

It was very dark that night. Soon it was impossible to see where they were going. Suddenly, and quite unexpectedly, Harriet found herself slithering down a grassy bank. Bert was taken by surprise too and with a startled cry he flew right over Harriet's head. There was a sudden, and mighty, SPLASH!

"Bert! What's happened?" cried Harriet in alarm.

"Gluggllgllugg . . ." There were sounds of someone spluttering. The moon appeared from behind the clouds for a brief moment and Harriet saw Bert sitting in the middle of a pond, with his knees under his chin and a startled Dizzy sitting on his head.

"Oh Bert . . . how could you? It's so undignified," she said, unaware of how undignified she looked herself sitting on her haunches in a patch of dandelions.

"Where is Dizzy?" asked Bert anxiously, when he had got out of the pond.

"I'm here," called Dizzy.

"Where?" Bert could hear Dizzy but couldn't see him.

"Up here," called Dizzy, trying to hold on as Bert searched around for him on the ground.

"Up where?" As Bert looked upwards, Dizzy slipped down the back of his head and before Dizzy even had time to shout he found himself sliding into the darkness inside Bert's shirt.

"Ha . . . ha . . . ha . . ." laughed Bert. "I'm being tickled."

"Bert . . . help!" Dizzy tried to make himself heard but his voice was muffled by the wet shirt. The more Dizzy tried to protect himself the more he tickled Bert. The more he tickled Bert the more Bert laughed. The more Bert laughed the more Dizzy wriggled.

"Really," snorted Harriet "If there is something to laugh about I wish someone would tell me what it is."

Bert managed to get his hand up the back of his shirt. "I've got it! I've got it!" he shouted. "Now let's see what is doing all that tickling. Dizzy! How did you get in there?" he gasped.

When Dizzy explained, Bert laughed so much that Dizzy began to laugh too. Even Harriet began to smile.

Bert was still laughing as he pushed Harriet up the grassy slope and onto the road they had so unceremoniously left.

Their relief knew no bounds when they saw the caravan standing in the moonlight.

"Home at last," sighed Dizzy happily.

"It wasn't lost at all!" said Harriet. "Of course I knew exactly where it was. I was just testing your sense of direction. I must say, it wasn't very good."

Bert and Dizzy stared at her in amazement, and then began to laugh all over again.

Mud

High on the moors the tracks were stony and the wind blew hard. Harriet didn't like being on the moors. She complained all the time.

"The caravan is too heavy . . . you should oil the wheels . . . my feet are sore . . . the wind is making my teeth ache . . . I've got a stone in my shoe . . ." But more than anything else she disliked the way the tracks twisted and turned. "Why can't they go straight like other roads?" she said.

"There must be a reason," said Dizzy from his place under the caravan.

"Rubbish!" said Harriet. "What do you know about such things?"

"More than you!" retorted Dizzy.

"No you don't!"

"Yes I do!"

"Please don't quarrel," said Bert.

"I'm not quarrelling, it's that frog who is quarrelling," snapped Harriet. She pressed her lips together tightly and glared straight ahead.

Bert got down and walked beside her. He turned up his coat collar and put his hands deep in his pockets.

At the next twist in the track Harriet ground her teeth together.

"I'll show them, and this silly road," she muttered to herself. And before Bert had any idea of what she was thinking she stepped off the edge of the track and onto the heathery moor.

Bumpety-bump went the caravan, because wherever Harriet went, of course the caravan had to follow.

Splish-splosh went the water in Dizzy's bucket.

"Ooooer!" Splash! went Dizzy as he shot up into the air and dropped back into the bucket.

"Harriet!" shouted Bert. "What do you think you are doing? Stop it! Stop it at once!" He tried to pull her back but when it came to strength he was no match for Harriet. And she had decided she was going to walk in a straight line . . . she was going to turn no more corners. She was very pleased with herself.

"You'll be sorry you did that!" shouted Dizzy from under the caravan. His bucket was swinging like a pendulum. It was making him feel sick. "You'll be sorry!"

"Frogs don't know anything!" scoffed Harriet.

"Neither do horses!" shouted Dizzy.

Bert had dug his heels in and was pulling with all his might.

"Stop! Stop!" he shouted.

"I can't hear what you're saying so you might just as well stop telling me to stop," said Harriet.

Bert didn't know what to do, and then quite suddenly Harriet stopped on her own. It happened so suddenly Bert almost lost his balance.

"Look at her feet," gasped Dizzy. Bert looked. Harriet was already looking at them. Her feet were sinking into the muddy ground. The mud was creeping up her legs.

Harriet looked at Bert. And Bert looked at Harriet. Her eyes were as big as saucers.

"Help me Bert," she said.

As fast as Bert pulled one of her legs free, he had to put it down to pull another one free. And each time he put a leg down it sank back into the mud. She was stuck fast.

Dizzy was hopping about excitedly. "We've got to get her out of there before she sinks altogether," he said. "You'll have to unhitch her from the caravan."

"Please hurry!" said Harriet. "I'm frightened."

They all were.

Without the weight of the caravan pulling her down Bert managed to free Harriet's legs from the mud and lead her back onto the stony track.

"Ugh!" said Harriet, looking at her legs and wrinkling her nose. "Will someone get this horrible stuff off my legs?"

But Bert was looked at something else. The caravan had tipped over at a crazy angle and now it too was sinking into the mud.

"That's my home," said Bert sadly, "and now I'm going to lose it."

"Not if I can help it," said Dizzy and with two bounds had disappeared into the heather.

"I knew you couldn't rely on frogs," said Harriet sadly. "Always hop away when there's trouble."

Bert ignored her. He knew Dizzy would be back.

There was a coil of rope hanging at the back of the caravan. With Harriet holding onto the back of his coat with her teeth so that he wouldn't fall into the mud himself Bert managed to unhook it. He made a loop and was trying to throw it round one of the caravan shafts when Dizzy returned accompanied by a crowd of other frogs.

"This isn't a party you know," said Harriet icily. The frogs ignored her completely.

"Cut as much heather as you can," said Dizzy.

As fast as Bert cut the heather the frogs dragged it onto the mud. They were too light to sink into it themselves. Soon there was a carpet of heather all round the caravan.

"Now you can tie the rope on," said Dizzy. "Step carefully."

"Don't do it!" whinnied Harriet as Bert stepped cautiously onto the heather. "It's a trick! You'll sink!" But Bert didn't sink. He tied the rope securely and returned to the stony ground.

"Now it's Harriet's turn," said Dizzy. "Tie the rope to her harness Bert. When I give the signal everyone must push and pull at the same time."

Bert went round to the back of the caravan and got ready to push. The frogs positioned themselves behind the wheels.

"Now!" shouted Dizzy.

Harriet pulled as hard as she possibly could. She wanted to help. She knew it was her fault the caravan was stuck in the mud.

Slowly the caravan began to move. With a last heave, and a last push, and a loud squelch! it bumped up onto the stony track. It was safe.

"Three cheers for the frogs!" shouted Bert throwing his hat into the air with a joyful whoop.

"Hooray!" whinnied Harriet before she could stop herself.

Pollen

They had liked the look of the meadow from the moment they first saw it, so they had stopped. Now Bert was lying in the sun tickling his chin with a buttercup and looking at the sky. Harriet was chomping at the grass and Dizzy had gone off exploring.

"Atishoo!"

"Who was that?" Bert rolled over and looked around.

"Aaa . . . it's me . . . Aaatishoo!" said Dizzy.

"Are you getting a cold?" asked Bert.

"Frogs don't get colds."

"Then why are you sneezing?"

"I don't know. Atishoo! I hoped you would be able to tell me. Atishoo! I do wish I could stop."

"Try holding your breath," said Bert.

Dizzy did. Until his face was purple. Then he let out a sneeze even bigger and louder than the one before.

"What's the matter with him?" asked Harriet.

"Only a horse . . . Atishoo! . . . would ask such a silly . . . Atishoo! . . . question . . . Atishoo!" said Dizzy between sneezes.

"Sorry I asked," said Harriet taking offence and walking away with her nose in the air.

"Atishoo! Atishoo! Atishoo!" The harder Dizzy tried to stop the more he sneezed. "Atishoo! Atishoo! Atishoo!"

"Perhaps it's the sun," said Bert. He picked Dizzy up and carried him, still sneezing into the caravan. It was cool and dark away from the bright sunlight. Bert put Dizzy on the table then sat and watched and waited. They were both beginning to feel hopeful, when, "Atishoo!"

To Bert's astonishment and Dizzy's complete confusion, the sneeze threw Dizzy into two backward somersaults and then straight into a bag of flour which was standing open on a shelf.

"A . . . a . . . tishoo!" The flour flew from the bag in a white cloud, in the middle of which was Dizzy.

Dizzy landed on the table. He didn't know what had happened. His nose was full of flour. His eyes were full of flour. His ears were full of flour. He hopped round and round the table like a cloud on legs. He looked so funny Bert could only laugh helplessly.

"Help! Help! Atishoo! Help! Atishoo!" As Dizzy's voice grew fainter the sneezes grew louder and stronger. All Dizzy could think of was to get to his bucket. By luck, and certainly not by good judgement, because he couldn't see a thing, he jumped off the table, onto the floor and through the door in two leaps.

"Atishoo! Atishoo!" Dizzy bounced about over the grass like a jumping bean. He didn't know which way to go, or where he was heading. Where was his bucket?

Bert tried to direct him between gasps of laughter but with ears full of flour Dizzy couldn't hear him. Though Dizzy didn't know it he was bouncing straight towards Harriet. He bumped against her legs.

Harriet looked down and started with horror as she saw the white thing hopping about between her legs. As it hopped under her tummy and towards her back legs she put her own head between her legs to see where it was going, and what it was doing. She looked as though she was about to turn a somersault herself.

Bert laughed so much the tears rolled down his face. He had to hold his tummy, it ached so. He tried to say, "Don't tread on him," but it came out, "d . . . d . . . d . . . d . . . d . . ."

If he had been able to see, Dizzy would never have dared get so close to Harriet's feet. As it was, he didn't know where he was, and quite by accident he bounced up and hit her right on the nose.

Harriet panicked. She closed her eyes tightly. But instead of standing still as she usually did when she closed her eyes she began to leap and bound too, trying to get away from the thing.

There was Dizzy, unable to see, even with his eyes open, hopping about like a mad jumping bean. He could feel the thud of hooves all around him. He was panicking too.

And there was Harriet, unable to see because her eyes were closed, crying for help and jumping about like a bucking bronco. How Dizzy wasn't trodden on and squashed flat Bert never knew. But thankfully, he wasn't.

Bert tried to catch hold of Harriet's tail to stop her, but that only frightened her the more, and he had to let go. He lay on the grass panting and laughing.

"I should get out of the way if I were you. She's going to tread on you if you don't." Bert looked up just in time to roll to one side as Harriet came thudding past.

"What are you doing down here anyway," asked a voice in his ear. It was Dizzy. Still sneezing, but able to hear and see because he had sneezed most of the loose flour off his little green body. "And what is she doing?" he asked.

Bert explained. Dizzy gulped and if he hadn't been covered in flour Bert would have seen him go pale.

"We've got to stop her somehow," said Bert as Harriet thudded towards them again and they both scrambled for safety. Dizzy under the fence and Bert over it.

But nothing they tried worked, so they sat on the fence and waited for her to get tired. Every time Dizzy sneezed, he fell to the ground, and Bert had to put him back on the post.

Then, when Harriet was thudding straight towards them and they were trying to decide which way to jump, she opened her eyes and slid to a halt.

"Why am I running?" she asked sweetly. "Am I running away from something? I really don't remember."

Before either of them could think of anything to say Dizzy sneezed again.

"Why doesn't he wipe that pollen off his nose?" said Harriet.

Bert looked at Dizzy's nose. It was yellow like buttercup pollen. Dizzy tried to look at his nose himself.

"Buttercup pollen always makes frogs sneeze," said Harriet.

"Does it?" said Dizzy. "I didn't know that." Neither did Harriet, she's just made it up, but it sounded right.

"Hop into your bucket and wash it off," said Bert.

"Oh, don't do that," said Harriet in her best aunty voice, "that will only make it go hard, then you'll never get it off."

"Really?" said Dizzy.

"Really!" said Harriet, as though it was true. And of course it might have been so Dizzy and Bert took no chances.

Bert found a small paint brush and cleaned Dizzy with that. It tickled Dizzy and made him laugh. But it did get the pollen off. And when the pollen was gone he stopped sneezing.

"That will teach you to go sticking your nose into buttercups," said Harriet. "Now, can you tell me why I was running like that?"

Of course Dizzy could, but he didn't dare tell her. And he made Bert promise not to tell her either. He had the feeling that the less she knew about that adventure the better it would be for all of them, but specially for him.

Waves

"There it is," said Bert.

"There's what?" asked Harriet.

"The sea of course," said Bert.

They had stopped to give Harriet a rest, and there in the distance between two hills, was the sea.

"Will we get any closer?" said Harriet.

"We'll get right to the very edge," said Bert.

"It won't fall on us will it?" said Harriet. There seemed to be rather a lot of it.

"Of course not," laughed Bert.

Dizzy was asleep in his bucket under the caravan otherwise he would have had a few questions to ask too.

They were right beside the sea before Dizzy woke. Harriet was watching the waves break over the beach with a mixture of wonder and fear. She didn't know what to make of it.

Dizzy hopped from his bucket. He could smell things watery and fishy. "Where are we?" he asked, bobbing up and down with excitement. "And what's all that water?"

"The sea, of course," said Bert, very surprised at the question.

"What's the sea?" said Dizzy, surprising him even more.

Before Bert could answer Dizzy was bounding towards the waves.

"Stop! Stop!" shouted Bert. There was something Dizzy should know about the sea. But he was too late.

"Shan't be long," shouted Dizzy. "I'm going for a swim."

And in he dived.

"Oh dear," sighed Bert.

No sooner was Dizzy in the sea than he was out again, and hopping as fast as he could up the beach.

"What's wrong with him?" asked Harriet in astonishment as Dizzy dived into his bucket and began splashing wildly.

"Ugh! Ugh!" he was saying . . . "Get it off . . . get it off . . ."

Bert waited until the splashing had finished. "Are you alright now?" he asked.

"Why didn't someone tell me it was salty?" said Dizzy. "I'm a fresh water frog . . . I can't bear to be near anything salty . . . Ugh!" Even the thought of it made him shudder.

"You didn't give anyone a chance to tell you," said Bert.

Harriet wanted to take a closer look at the sea herself. Anything wet that could upset a frog that much was worth taking a closer look at. Bert unhitched her from the caravan and she went down to the water's edge.

"Come away from there!" shouted Dizzy. "It's salty. You won't like it."

Harriet pretended she hadn't heard. And anyway, she quite liked the taste of salt. She let the edge of a wave ripple round her feet. She liked the way it felt. She went a little deeper.

"You'd better stop her," said Dizzy from the safety of his bucket. "She'll get the taste of it in a minute. She won't like it. She'll bolt and then we'll never catch her."

"Don't worry so much," said Bert with a smile. "She knows what she is doing."

Harriet didn't bolt, but she did gallop backwards and forwards along the beach through the edge of the waves. Her feet threw up a cloud of sparkling spray that made her feel she was in a dream.

Bert sat on the sand and watched her. He had never seen her so happy. Dizzy came and sat beside him and they talked about this, and that, and Bert told Dizzy stories of when he was young.

When the sun went down and it was time to leave the beach and find somewhere to stop for the night, Harriet was as fresh as a daisy. She said her gallop in the sea had made her feel like a young filly again.

"I didn't know you had been young," said Dizzy cheekily. "When was that then?"

Harriet looked at him steadily. "You can't upset me today," she said. "I even like frogs today. I can even understand why you like water so much."

"I don't like the salty kind," said Dizzy, and shuddered as he remembered the feel of it on his skin and the taste of it in his mouth.

"Oh well," said Harriet. "Horses always have had more sense than frogs."

Then she plodded off happily into the sunset and Dizzy settled happily into his very own bucket of fresh clear water that hadn't a trace of salt in it.